DATE DUE

THE CHICAGO PUBLIC LIBRARY

DISCARD

THE CHICAGO PUBLIC LIBRARY
WEST PULLMAN BRANCH
800 W. 119TH STREET
CHICAGO, IL 60643

**MADE IN THE U.S.A.**

# Music CDs
## From Start to Finish

**Mindi Rose Englart**
**Photographs by Peter Casolino**

BLACKBIRCH PRESS, INC.
WOODBRIDGE, CONNECTICUT

For Noah Elliot Roffman—future blues artist

Published by Blackbirch Press, Inc.
260 Amity Road
Woodbridge, CT 06525

e-mail: staff@blackbirch.com
Web site: www.blackbirch.com

©2001 by Blackbirch Press, Inc.
First Edition

All rights reserved. No part of this book may be reproduced in any form without permission in writing from Blackbirch Press, Inc., except by a reviewer.

Printed in the United States

10 9 8 7 6 5 4 3 2 1

**Photo Credits:** All photographs ©Peter Casolino, except cover background, ©Bruce Glassman; page 3, ©Photodisc; page 9 (right), Barry Tenin; pages 19, 27, 29, ©The Image Works; page 26, courtesy Library of Congress.

**Library of Congress Cataloging-in-Publication Data**
Englart, Mindi Rose.
Music CDs: from start to finish / by Mindi Rose Englart.
   p.   cm. — (Made in the U.S.A.)
   Summary: From setting up the studio to packaging the finished product, looks at the steps involved in recording and producing a compact disc.
   ISBN 1-56711-485-7
   1. Compact discs. 2. Sound—Recording and reproducing. [1. Compact discs. 2. Sound—Recording and reproducing.] I. Title. II. Series.
TK7882.C56 E54 2001
621.389'32—dc21                              2001002568

## Contents

| | |
|---|---|
| At the Studio | 5 |
| Arranging to Record | 6 |
| Preparing the Studio | 7 |
| The Band Arrives | 8 |
| Jug Bands | 9 |
| The Band Sets Up | 10 |
| "Take" One | 13 |
| Overdubbing | 14 |
| The Band "Wraps Up" | 16 |
| What Is a CD? | 18 |
| Preparing to Mix | 21 |
| Improving the Mix | 22 |
| The "Mix Down" | 24 |
| Recording the Master | 25 |
| Analog and Digital Recording | 26 |
| Packaging | 28 |
| Duping and Production | 29 |
| Let There Be Music! | 31 |
| | |
| Glossary | 32 |
| For More Information | 32 |
| Index | 32 |

What do video games, pop music, and computer software have in common? They're all recorded onto compact discs, or CDs. CDs, and DVDs (digital versatile discs), are the latest and most efficient way to record information.

CDs are everywhere today. That's because they are easy to store and inexpensive to make. They also hold a lot of data, and the sound and visual quality is very high. If you have a computer and a CD-R drive, you can even create your own CDs.

What are CDs made out of? How do they get produced? Let's see how a professional music CD gets made.

*CDs are everywhere today.*

Living Sound →

*Jeff Jacoby runs Living Sound recording studio.*

## A Busy Studio

Living Sound Productions is a recording studio in Bethany, Connecticut. The owner and recording engineer, Jeff Jacoby, produces programs for film and television. He also records and produces radio spots, concerts, and CDs.

Jeff is also the executive producer of "The Traveling Radio Show." This educational program presents stories about people and places from around America.

# Arranging to Record

Living Sound Productions has agreed to record a CD for a band called Washboard Slim and the Blue Lights. Jeff will be both the producer and the engineer. As producer, he will supervise the recording process. As engineer, he is responsible for all technical parts of the recording.

*Jeff calls the band to schedule their recording session.*

# Preparing the Studio

On the day of the session, Jeff prepares the studio. He sets up microphones and checks the sound levels on the equipment.

*Jeff sets up his equipment and microphones.*

*Above:* Band members unpack their equipment. *Inset:* Jeff and the band plan the session.

# The Band Arrives

When Jeff finishes his preparation, the band members arrive with their instruments. This band of five people may use more than 12 instruments during the recording session.

## "Jug Bands"

Bands such as The Grateful Dead and The Lovin' Spoonful started as jug bands. The Beatles started as a skiffle band (an English jug band).

Jug bands are famous for turning regular household items into musical instruments. They use many elements, including: drums, harmonica, washboard, kazoo, jug, washtub bass, banjo, guitar, steel guitar, piano, accordian, flutes, sitar, mandolin, pots, and pans. Sometimes, jug bands even use whoopie cushions and nose flutes!

**Clockwise:** A steel guitar; Washboard Slim and the Blue Lights are one of the few remaining jug bands in America today; special gloves (with thimbles on fingers) used to play the washboard.

# The Band Sets Up

Once they are in the studio, the band members take their instruments out of their protective cases. Each instrument is set up near a microphone that will best record its sound.

Band member Howard Horn unpacks and sets up his washtub bass.

*Bandleader Peter Menta sets up his washboard.* **Inset left:** *Tuning a slide guitar.* **Inset right:** *Accordian player Brooks Barnett gets comfortable with his instrument.*

The washboard player stays separate in a sound booth to isolate his sound.
**Inset:** Mat Kastner plays the banjo.

***Above:*** *The band warms up.* ***Right:*** *Jeff listens to the sound as the band records. The sound is recorded through the wires plugged into the "patch bay" at the back of the mixer.*

## "Take" One

After the band has warmed up, they begin to play. Each microphone is connected to a separate track on Jeff's mixer (part of the recording system). The mixer is first used to record each instrument on its own track. Later, the mixer will be used to "mix" all the tracks together and adjust the volume of each instrument as it is heard. Jeff is careful to keep checking each band member's microphone to make sure the sound comes through well. The band may play the same song over and over until they feel they have recorded it just right. Each try is called a "take."

*As the band plays, Jeff adjusts the levels (or volume) of sound on the mixer.*
**Opposite:** *The singer, Deirdre Menchaca, records onto a separate track for overdubbing.*

## Overdubbing

After Jeff has each sound assigned to a track, he may have a particular band member play just their part again. He may also have the singer sing onto a separate track. Later, he will overdub. That means he'll layer these sounds on top of the other tracks. This will give the music a "fuller" sound.

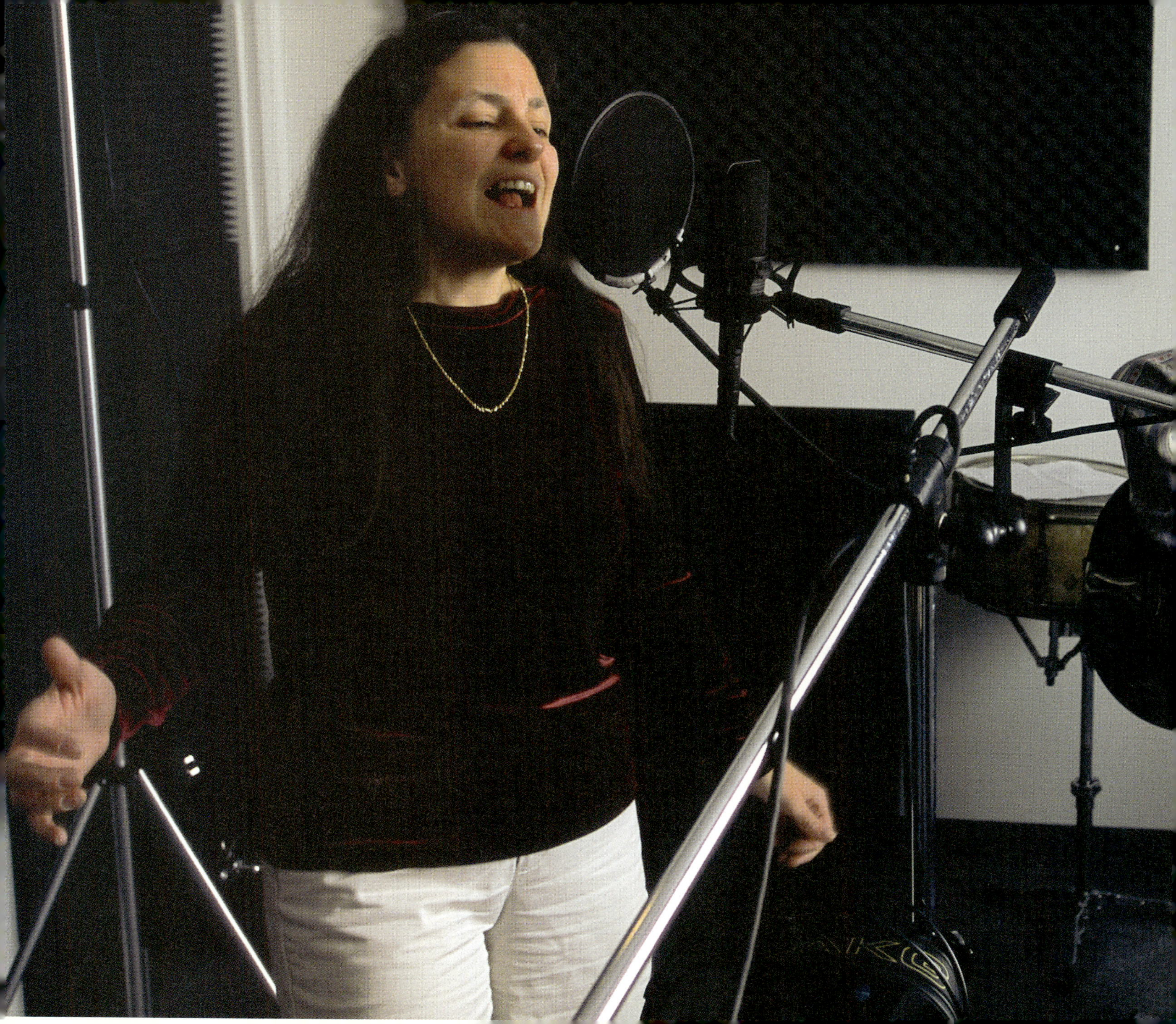

# The Band "Wraps Up"

Jeff and Peter go over the recording very carefully. They want to make sure they have all the songs and additional tracks needed to make the best mix for the final CD.

After a long, tiring day in the studio, the band packs up.

17

# What Is a CD?

A CD is a thin piece of plastic, about 1.2 millimeters thick. During manufacturing, millions of tiny bumps are pressed into the plastic. These bumps are arranged in a very long spiral. The disc is then coated with a thin metal layer and a protective acrylic layer.

## DID YOU KNOW?

- Since their release in 1982, compact discs have taken the world by storm. In 1983, more than 800,000 discs were sold. By 1997, this number had grown to more than 753 million discs worldwide. Today, CDs account for nearly 90% of all music sales. This expansion makes the compact disc industry one of the fastest growing industries of all time.
- If you could take the data track off a CD and stretch it into a straight line, it would be almost 3.5 miles long!
- There are over 783 million bytes (bits of data) on a CD.

**Opposite:** This machine applies a protective coating of acrylic to CDs during the manufacturing process.

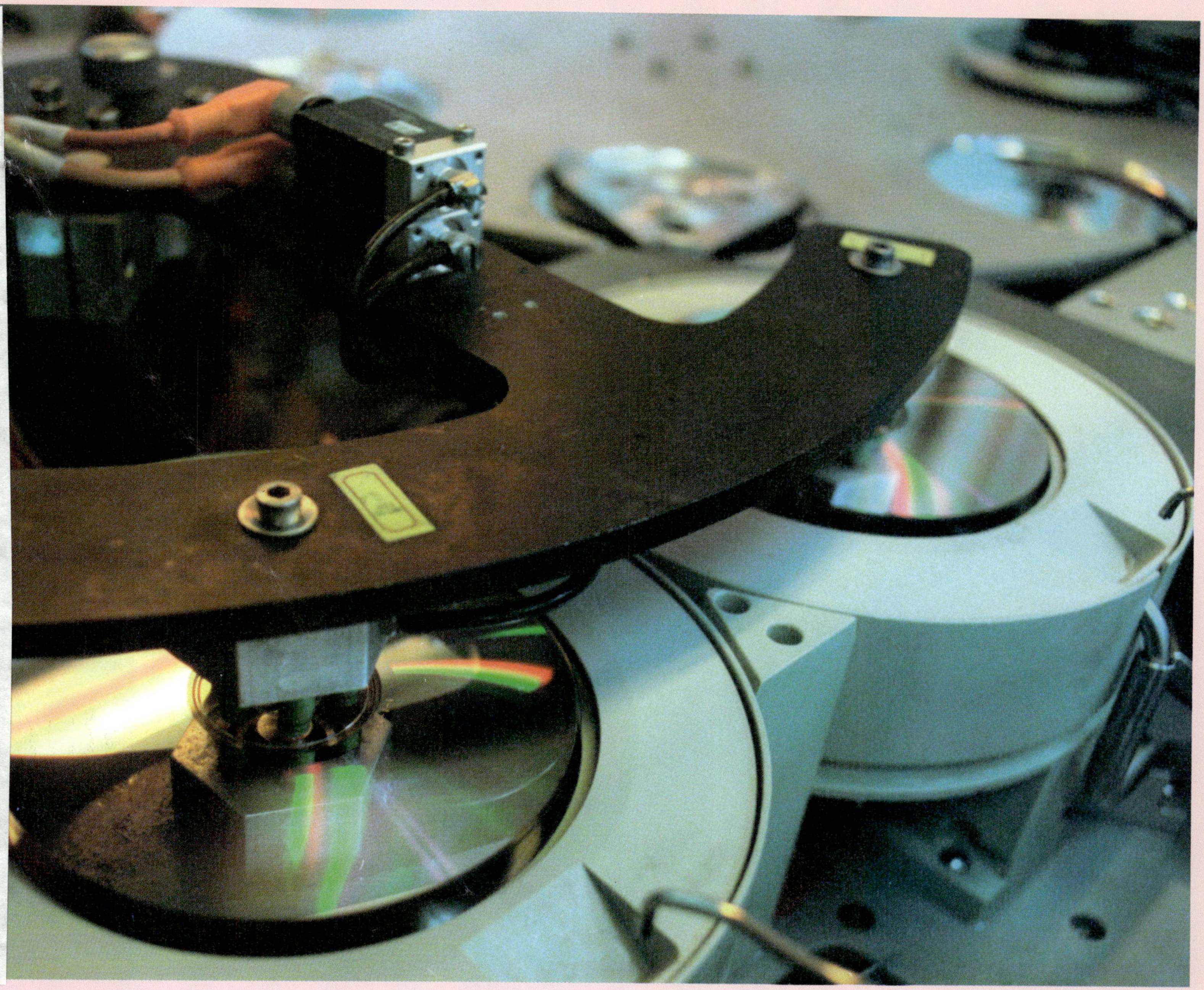

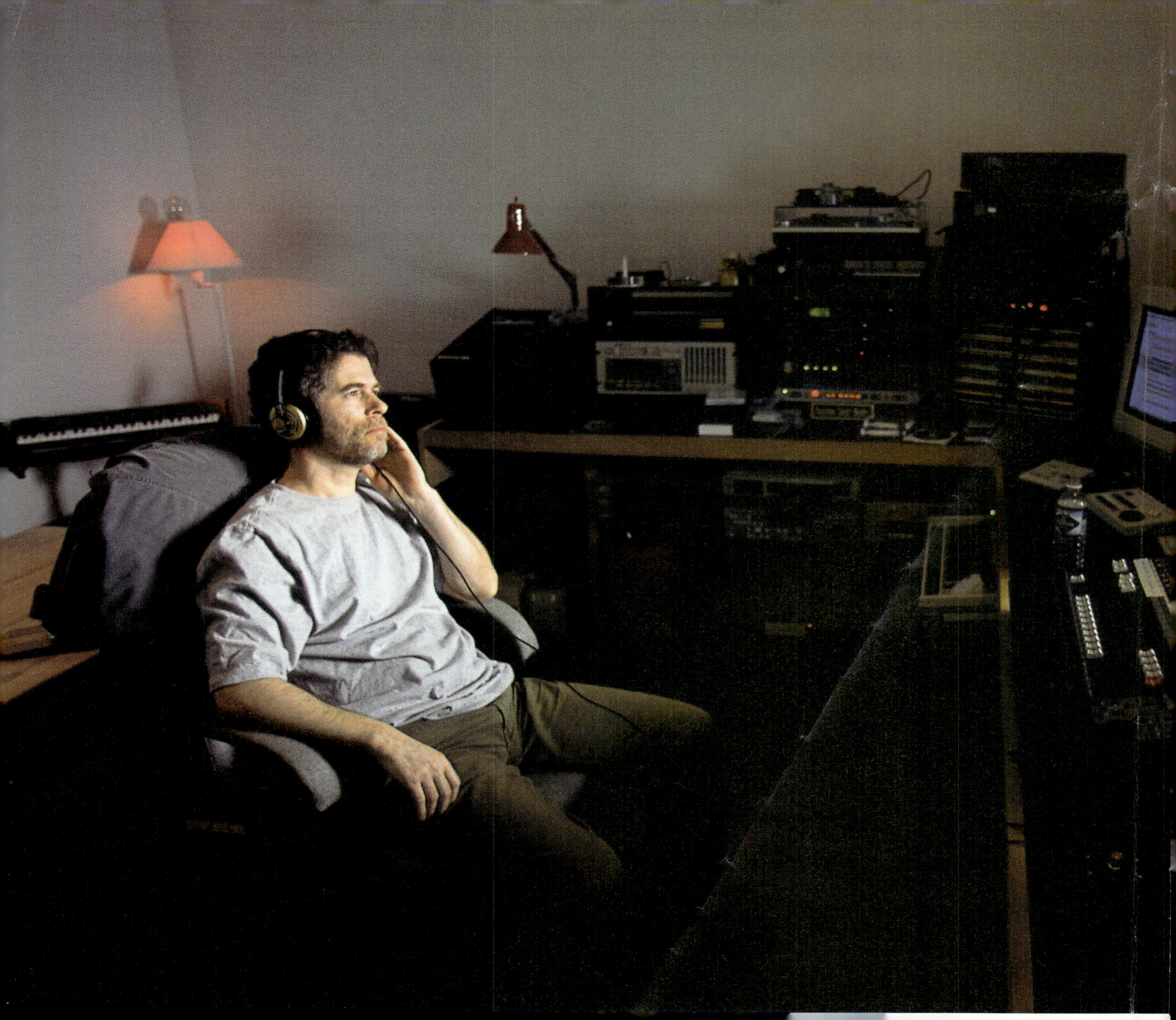

## Preparing to Mix

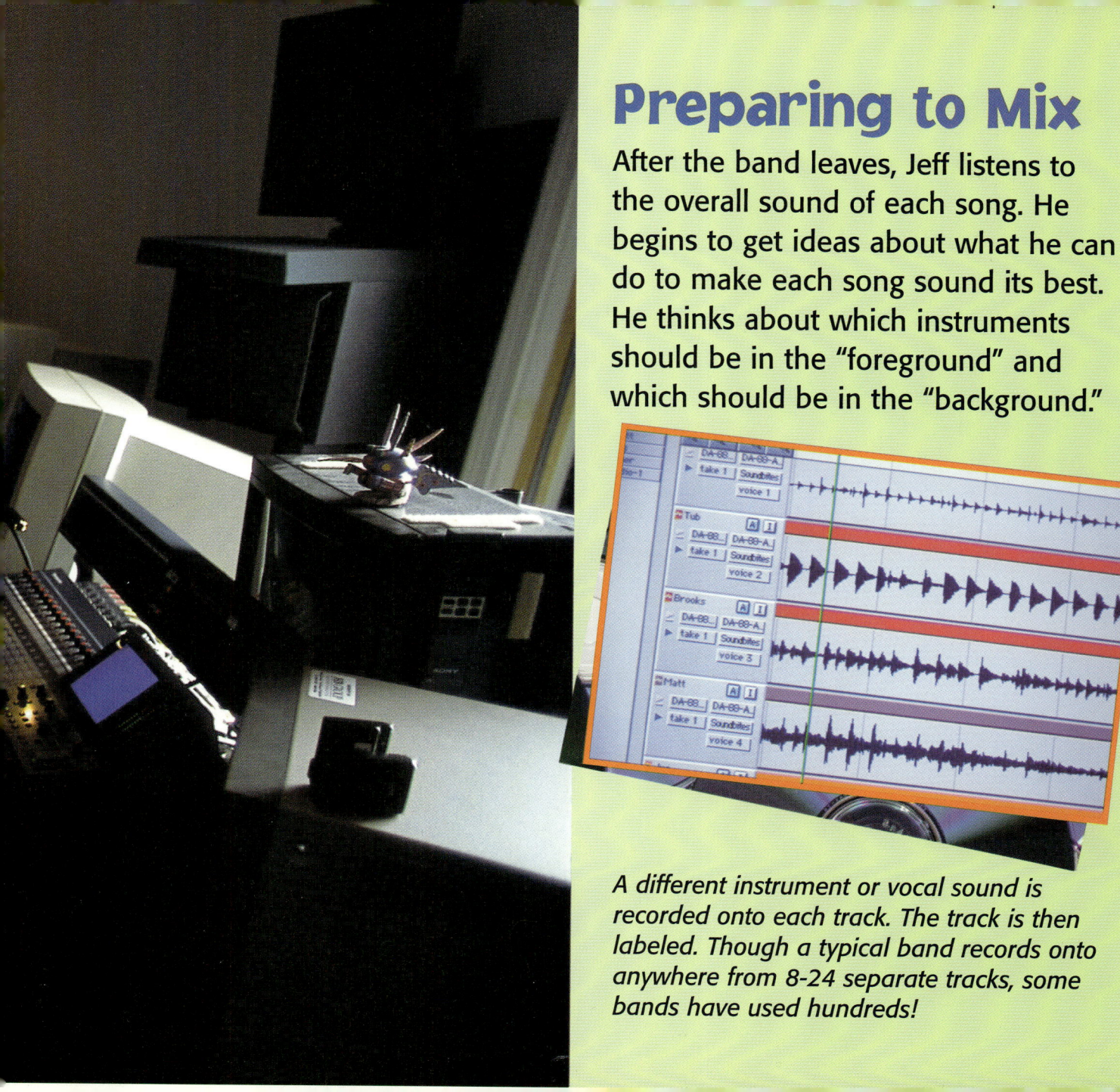

After the band leaves, Jeff listens to the overall sound of each song. He begins to get ideas about what he can do to make each song sound its best. He thinks about which instruments should be in the "foreground" and which should be in the "background."

*A different instrument or vocal sound is recorded onto each track. The track is then labeled. Though a typical band records onto anywhere from 8-24 separate tracks, some bands have used hundreds!*

# Improving the Mix

A recording engineer has hundreds of ways to adjust sound. Here are a few examples:
- Volume: Using the faders (shown below), the engineer can adjust the loudness of each track. This is called "setting levels."
- Stereo Field: "Panning" moves sound from left to right between speakers.

*Jeff uses a variety of special effects with fun names like: flanging, phasing, echo, delays, limiting, modulation, and tremolo.*

For example, when you listen to a CD, you may hear more guitar sound from the left speaker, and more singing from the right. This technique can help a recording sound best to the human ear.
- Equalizing: Lower frequencies are called "bass" and higher frequencies are called "treble." Adjusting frequencies can make a sound stand out. A good mix usually covers a wide range of frequencies.
- Signal processing: Effects, such as reverberation and echo, can have a big impact on the sound of the music.

**Left:** Jeff adjusts the reverberation (reverb), which can make the recording sound like it was recorded in a bigger or smaller room. **Right:** All outputs and inputs in the special effects machine go through a patch bay.

*Professional mixing boards can have hundreds of tracks and controls.*

# The Mix Down

At this point, the engineer can really change the sound of the entire band. As he mixes, Jeff will play a song over and over, listening carefully. He makes changes that are saved with a feature called "automation." Automation records and plays back each set of changes to the mix. When he has a final mix, Jeff records it back onto the computer in stereo. That's called the "mix down."

# Recording the Master

Once Jeff has the final mix of each song in stereo, he can apply effects to a whole song at once. He then arranges the order of the songs and the amount of pause between songs. Then he "burns", or records, a finished master CD.

*Jeff finishes and "burns" the master CD.*

# Analog and Digital Recording

In 1877, Thomas Edison created the first device for recording and playing back sounds. To use Edison's original phonograph, a person spoke while a tin foil cylinder was rotated. A needle scratched grooves onto the cylinder.

To play the sound back, the needle moved over the grooves scratched during recording. During playback, the grooves pressed into the tin caused the needle to vibrate—to play the sound. This series of grooves is called an analog wave—it represents the vibrations that a sound creates.

*Portrait of Thomas Edison at work on his phonograph.*

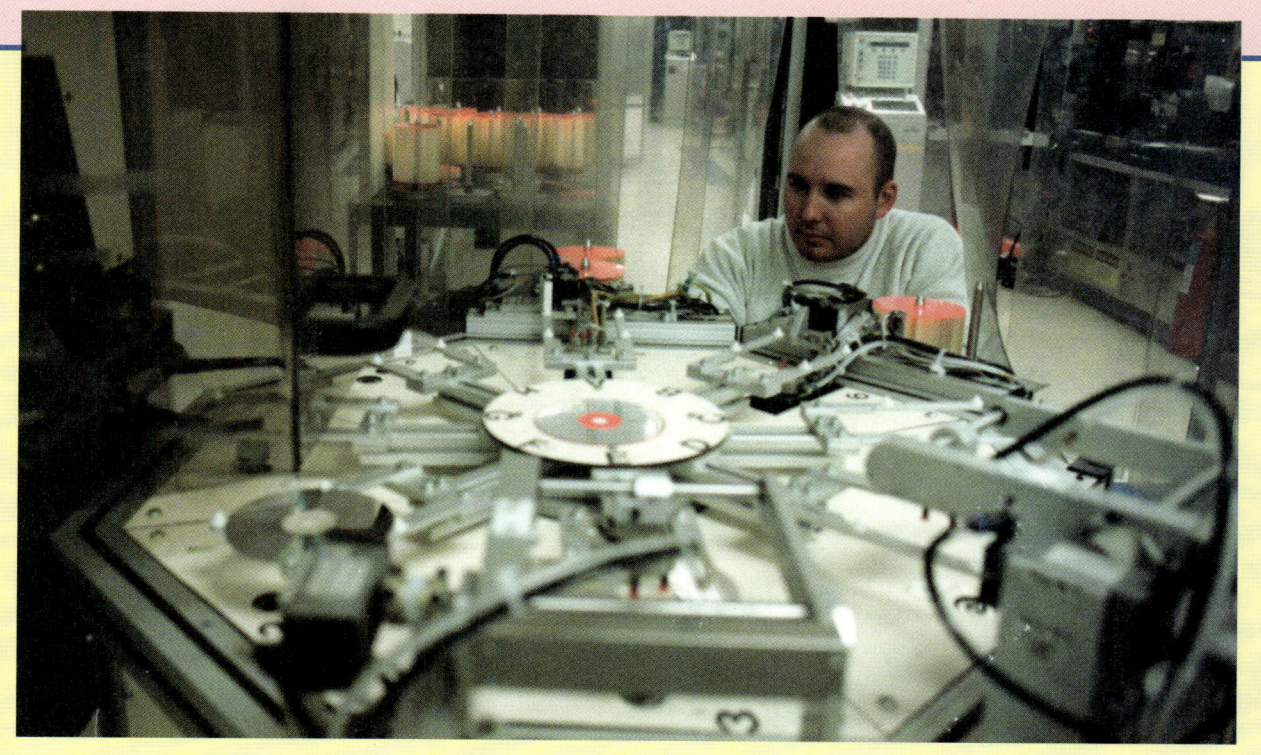

*A worker at a CD production machine.*

    Digital recording changes an analog wave into a stream of numbers. It then records the numbers instead of the wave. This conversion is done by a device called an analog-to-digital converter. To play back the music, the stream of numbers is converted back to an analog wave by a digital-to-analog converter (DAC). The analog wave produced by the DAC is amplified and fed into speakers so you can hear the sound.

A graphic designer works on ideas for a CD cover.
**Inset:** A photographer takes a picture of the band to go inside the CD cover.

## Packaging

As copies of the master CD are being manufactured, a graphic artist creates an eye-catching CD cover to put into the CD case, or "jewel-box."

28

# Duping and Production

Jeff sends the master CD to a duplication plant (often called a duping house). Here, workers use special machines to create many CDs from the master CD. The CDs are printed with a label, and packaged in CD jewel-boxes for shipping.

*A worker stacks raw CDs onto a spindle. Next, they will go through a CD recording machine.*

**Want to hear a song from the finished CD? Visit our web site at: www.blackbirch.com**

# Let There Be Music!

After the CD has been made, it is distributed for sale. You can find CDs in music stores, at concerts, in radio stations, and in homes around the world.

*A disc jockey at WPKN in Bridgeport, Connecticut, plays a song from the Washboard Slim and the Blue Lights CD.*

31

# Glossary

**Amplify** to make something louder.

**Frequency** the number of cycles per second of a radio wave.

**Jewel box** a plastic case that holds a CD.

**Mandolin** a small, guitar-like instrument that has metal strings.

**Reverberate** when a sound echoes loudly and repeatedly.

**Take** each time a band plays a song for recording.

**Track** several paths along which music is recorded on magnetic tape.

# For More Information

**Books**

Ardley, Neil. *Eyewitness: Music*. NY: DK Publishing, 2000.

Barrons. *Music and Sound* (Modern Media Series). Hauppauge, NY: Barrons Educational Series, 2000.

Sproule, Anna. *Thomas A. Edison: The World's Greatest Inventor* (Giants of Science). Woodbridge, CT: Blackbirch Press, Inc., 2000.

**Web Sites**

***Washboard Slim and the Blue Lights***
www.washboardslim.com

***Information on music recording, production, and publishing***
www.emigroup.com

# Index

Beatles, 9
Bethany, CT, 5
"Burn," 25
Duping, 29
Edison, Thomas, 26
Graphic artist, 28
Grateful Dead, 9
Jacoby, Jeff, 5-7, 13-14, 16, 21, 24
Jug bands, 9
Living Sound Productions, 5-6
Lovin' Spoonful, The, 9
Mix, 21-24
Packaging, 28
Phonograph, 26
Recording, 6, 8, 13, 26-27
Software, 3
Songs, 25
Take, 13
"The Traveling Radio Show," 5
Track, 13-14, 16
Video games, 3
Washboard Slim and the Bluelights, 6, 9
What Is a CD?, 18

THE CHICAGO PUBLIC LIBRARY